Dark
Needs

A Dark Light of Day Novella

T.M. FRAZIER

ISBN-13:

978-1507828564

ISBN-10: 150782856X

Cover Design by Sara Eirew

DEDICATION

For Clarissa, Julie, and Kimmi

CONTENTS

ACKNOWLEDGMENTS

Thank you to everyone who believes in me, especially my readers. Your messages and support mean everything to me. When I first wrote The Dark Light of Day I never thought it would become anything more than just a story I wrote. It was all of you who turned it into more than I could have ever imagined.

Thank you to all the bloggers who took the time to read, review, and share Jake & Abby's story with their followers. Maryse, Aestas, YaYa, S&M Book Obsessions, my Goodreads readers, and Milasy & Lisa over at The Rock Stars of Romance. What you do for writers and what you have done fore me and my work has been nothing short of amazing. I will forever be grateful to you.

This year wouldn't have been the same without the support of a very special friend of mine. Lea (Mistress L) from S&M Book Obsessions. Thank you for going above and beyond the book world for me. Thank you for your kind advice and words of encouragement from the very first moments of my pregnancy. I never thought someone I met on Twitter, someone whose first words to me went something like 'I love your hair, I want to scalp you and wear your head' would become such a great friend of mine and someone I would love very much.

Thank you to the author friends turned real life friends that I have made during this journey. It's an odd but wonderful feeling to be both a friend and a fan. Aurora Rose

Reynolds, Rochelle Paige, Tessa Teevan, Monica Robinson, Pam Godwin, Ella Fox, Joanna Wylde, Harper Sloan, Penelope Ward, and so many more, your talent and your success inspires me to keep going every single day. Thank you for being there for me when I needed you. I know your time is valuable, thank you for spending some of it on me.

Thank you to my husband Logan. It's been a crazy fucking year, babe! Thank you for always supporting my dreams and for not looking at me like I'm psychotic when I ask you about crazy book scenarios, but instead countering with your own crazy ideas. Thank you for taking an interest in what I love. Thank you for loving my book world and the people in it. Thank you for loving your crazy wife, and trust me, I DO know that I can be fucking crazy.

Most of all, thank you for rubbing my back, holding my hand, playing music on my belly, telling me how beautiful I am (even though it was far from the truth), binge eating Oreos with me, running the bath for me, sleeping on the couch with me when I was too uncomfortable to sleep in our bed, and for crying tears of joy with me when we heard that first beautiful scream. Thank you for our new baby girl. Charley is so lucky to have you as her Daddy. I love you to the moon and back, forever and ever and ever. There is no one else I would rather journey through this life with.

Thank you to my baby girl, Charley. You are the most perfect little thing that has ever happened to us. Mommy loves you unconditionally, and you are never never ever allowed to read any of my books!

ONE

Jake

Owen didn't know who he was really running from when he took off from Coral Pines. In his mind he was probably escaping the police and his imminent incarceration for the shooting of my daughter.

What he was really running from was his imminent death.

I'd been up for three days straight but felt as if I could've bench pressed a semi-truck and rowed across the Coral Pines River and back and still not have fully exerted myself.

I was fucking elated.

I was also scared out of my mind.

Over the years it was that lack of fear that helped me to be able to carry out my work, and do it well.

But when I stood on the rickety front porch of Bee's Nan's

9

house with one hand on the doorknob, I couldn't bring myself to turn it. I was frozen in fucking fear, unable to face what might happen behind that door once it opened.

What would Abby think of me when she came face to face with the blood that was literally still on my hands? When the reality of what I'd done, what I did, and what I would do again was right in front of her. What happens when 'Jake kills people' is no longer just an abstract idea?

Bee knew I was going to find and kill Owen, she encouraged me by showing me the pictures of the aftermath of Owen's vicious attack on her. She knew my blood would boil, and I would seek immediate revenge. When I turned that knob and Abby saw me, saw the bloody proof of who I really was staring her in the face and it all became real, would she still feel like she could accept that part of me? Would she still want me in her life? In Georgia's?

Abby loved me, for exactly who I was, fully knowing the devil lived inside me. Knowing of the brutality that was part of the deep seeded makeup of who I truly was.

It was easy to live with a theory, something that almost wasn't real because it wasn't something she had to deal with. It was entirely different to come face to face with the truth of it all.

Fuck.

I could've washed off the blood and pretended like I didn't murder the motherfucker who'd almost killed the only two people I would die a thousand times over for, that the evidence of what I'd done wasn't dried on my skin. It would have been easier that way, but only in the short term. My plans for Abby and Bee were long term. I didn't want to be clean when she saw me. I wanted to rip off the band-aid and take whatever was coming so we could move forward as a family.

My family.

Over and over again, Bee told me she loved me, But I needed her to see it.

I needed her to see me.

No matter who I'd killed in the past I'd never felt even the slightest bit sick about it, never even given it a second thought, but just the idea of losing Bee again made my fucking stomach roll.

I *never* should've left her.

But I was a fucking coward.

I *never* should've come back for her.

But I was a fucking coward.

I'd used a weak-as-shit rumor as my excuse to leave Bee because I was nothing but a weak, weak man who convinced himself whole heartedly that there was a possibility that it was true, that after our one perfect night together, she could go and fuck Owen, the boy next door/psycho rich kid.

What I was really doing was pushing Bee away before she got too close. Before she could really understand what made me tick and made the decision to leave me, I left her.

I've regretted it every second of every hour of every day since then.

For four years, I lived my life with my eyes closed and without Bee, because for the first time someone had the capability of actually hurting me instead of the other way around. So I used the bullshit rumor Owen's friend told me about Abby and Bee as my way to leave Coral Pines as quickly as my bike would take me before Bee had the chance to tear me apart at the seams.

The problem was that Bee was so fucking deep under my skin that every day she wasn't with me was a torture all it's own. But at the end of the day, I'd always thought that I'd done the right thing by her, by leaving, no matter the reason, because I knew she was better off without me.

I was positive I'd done the right thing for once in my life.

After four years, of the need to see her, talk to her, touch her, hadn't faded. It became stronger. So strong that my need for her was stronger than my need for anything else.

When it came down to it, I didn't come back because I thought she needed me. I came back because I was a selfish prick who couldn't stay the fuck away from her.

I loved her. Always had. Never thought I would be capable of that kind of love, but from the very moment I'd ripped that hoodie off her head in that junk yard and a beautiful pale faced red head stared up at me from the wrong side the barrel of my gun, I knew my life would never be the same.

It was because of her.

I didn't want to run, didn't want to live without her anymore.

So I decided not to.

I've doled out my fair share of torture, but none could've been more painful or cruel than the time I'd spent without Bee. I'd packed the saddle bags of my bike, days before I'd even heard of my father's death, and took off that very night.

I headed back to Coral Pines.

I was going back to get my girl.

I decided to stop being a pussy and just open the fucking door, when it swung wide open and I avoided a head injury by mere inches.

"Sorry, I heard your bike." Bee said, staring up at me with those wide eyes that I could get lost in all day every day. Her robe hung open, perky little rounded tits peeked out the top of her favorite Guns-N-Roses tank top, the tight shorts she always slept in left little to my imagination.

I'd spent a lot of time imagining when it came to Abby.

I stood my ground on the porch, feeling like this time I came in that I needed permission of some sort to cross into her house. "You're bleeding" Bee said, frantically patting me down, inspecting me for wounds.

"Bee, baby, look at me" I said, trying to get her attention. She kept going, kept looking for the source of the blood. Grabbing her arms, I held them down tightly to her sides, forcing her to look up at me. "Baby, it's not my blood" I assured her. Bee finally paused when she processed what I was trying to tell her. Much to my surprise she sighed with relief, slowly running the back of her hand down the side of my face, cradling my jaw in her palm.

This was it. This was when I fully expected her to turn and slam the fucking door in my face. If she didn't want me anymore I could at least live the rest of my pitiful life knowing she wouldn't have to be afraid of Owen.

At least I'd given that much to her.

Bee could reject me.

She could call me a monster and tell me she never wanted to see me again.

As much as I hated to admit it, even to myself, after four

13

years apart I'd moved way beyond a 'no'.

To be perfectly fucking honest...

I wasn't sure I could take no for an answer.

Bee didn't give me a chance to imagine what that kind of scenario it would look like because she placed her hand flat on my chest. "It's done?" she whispered.

I took a deep breath, "It's done, baby," I assured her.

And then she did it.

Something that put to rest all my inner dialogue about what she would do or how she would feel.

She smiled.

That smile reached from one ear to the other and was the most gut–twisting, fantastic thing I'd ever witnessed. "Tell me everything" Bee said, excitement flashed in her eyes.

She looked possessed.

She was hungry.

I was instantly hard.

I lifted Bee up into my arms and crushed my lips to hers. I'd waited way too fucking long for that kiss. Soft but demanding. Angry and passionate. A bit of heaven and a bit of hell. I put everything I ever wanted to tell her into that kiss. Every *I love you*, every *I'm sorry*, and every *thank you for loving me back* was said without words. I kicked the front door closed and carried Bee to her room. Pausing in the hallway, I gestured to the closed door across from Bee's.

"Georgia?" I mouthed.

"Fell asleep with her headphones on listening to Disney songs," Bee whispered, biting her lip.

I fucking LOVED my girl.

"Yay fucking Disney," I muttered.

What happened after that could only be described as frantic.

In her room, we tore at each other's clothes like our lives depended on being naked. It had been so long since I'd seen all of her. When I unhooked her bra and tossed it to the floor, I stepped back to admire my girl.

I know I'm a sick fuck, but her scars turned me on more now than they did during our first time together. They were a little less visible under her sleeve of tattoos, but they were there, and I couldn't help but step forward and trace my tongue around the deep red lines around her collar bone.

"My girl is so strong, so smart, and so fucking sexy" I spoke into her skin like I was talking directly to her scars, kissing and licking each and every one of them as I made my way to her shoulder and down her arm.

I was about to come in my pants like a twelve year old boy.

I needed Bee, and I was going to show her how very fucking much. I lunged at her, pressing my lips to hers, our mouths opening and our tongues mingling together like they were the ones fucking. I picked her up and carried her to the bed, tossing her onto the mattress and falling on top of her, our lips melded together, our bodies speaking to each other in a language that only two fucked-up people like ourselves could understand.

I'd always belonged to Bee, ever since that very first night. But right then, in her tiny bedroom in her Nan's house, years after we first met, she was finally going to be all mine, and I was going to make sure every part of her body knew who it belonged to.

MINE.

Never again would we ever be apart.

For the rest of my life, every day I drew breath, I would make fucking sure of it.

We unlatched from our kiss just long enough for to Bee to push my jeans down over my hips, getting on her knees to help pull them off my legs.

Owen's blood on her cheek.

"What?" she asked when she noticed I was staring. My woman was on her knees in front of me, blood from a life I took smeared on her face. I had an image flash through my brain of Bee's pink lips wrapped around my cock, and I almost blew my load right then.

At least, Owen had been good for something.

I made quick work of removing the rest of our clothes. Finally, there was nothing between us. Skin to skin. Hard on soft. My cock throbbed against her belly, dripping with need onto her skin as we clawed at one another, needing to be closer still.

I closed my eyes, wrapping my hand around the back of her neck, digging my fingers into her hair, holding her against me like at any moment I was going to realize that it was all just part of the dream I'd had every night since the day I left.

When I opened my eyes and looked down, my heart fluttered in my chest like a kid with a crush, because it was all real. She was there in the room with me. She wanted to be with me.

I think she still fucking loved me.

I set her back against the pillows and pushed her knees apart, spreading her legs so I could look upon what was mine. Her pussy glistened, waiting for me to stretch it open and fill it with my cock.

I needed to taste it.

I dove in fast, licking her from clit to rear and back again, flattening my tongue to get as much of her wetness in my mouth as possible. Bee shrieked in surprise, but quickly settled back against the pillows, gripping the sheets in her fists. Her moan vibrated against my tongue.

Since I was sure as shit I was going to hell and this was the only taste of heaven I was ever going to experience, so I was going to fucking take it.

Over and over again. For as long as she would let me.

Which I hoped would be forever.

Bee moaned again and fisted my hair, pulling on it as I lapped at her clit over and over again. Her thighs flailed on both sides of my face. The harder she pulled, the more turned on I got. I rubbed my cock against the mattress in an effort to find some sort of relief from the pain of my arousal. I pointed my tongue and drove it into her pussy. She arched her back and bit her lip, stifling a scream.

I decided right then and there that if I was ever put away on death row for any one of the many murders I'd carried out, the last meal I would request would be Bee's pussy.

I reached up and placed my hand over her lips to help quiet her, but instead of fighting me she sucked two of my fingers inside her mouth, rolling her tongue around them as I groaned onto her clit, the vibrations causing her to throw her head back and close her eyes. I pumped into her with two fingers from my other hand, groaning at the tightness of her pussy and was lost in the thought of her milking my cock the way she was milking my fingers right up until her tight little cunt clenched around them. Bee suddenly lifted her ass off the mattress and arched her back as she screamed through the greatest and most beautiful orgasm I'd ever witnessed, her pussy slowly pulsing its way back to earth.

"MY fucking pussy," I growled. "MINE."

Bee and I didn't do this the first time. I didn't have the chance to taste her back then, but I'd spent a great amount of time while we were apart thinking about it. Nothing in my imagination could even fathom what the taste of her orgasm on my tongue would like be in reality.

Bee's pussy tasted like sex wrapped in sunshine, rolled up in thousand dollar bills, and covered in powdered sugar.

Four years ago, when I took Bee's virginity, it was selfish of me. It was wrong. She was only seventeen and so vulnerable.

I would do it all over again every day for the rest of my fucking life.

Back then, I thought we would have all the time in the world. I thought we would have the chance to explore each other, experiment with what feels good, and generally fuck the shit out of each other until we were too tired to move, or until we fucking died.

Because frankly, I would gladly go to hell with my dick deep inside Bee.

Bee barely had a chance to find her way back into consciousness before I was between her legs, my hands on her knees, spreading her open in front of me, my cock ready to push into the most beautiful pink center I'd ever had the privilege of entering.

I grabbed my shaft to guide it home when Bee said something that made me pause. "Will it hurt this time?" she asked, panting. Her little nipples stood at attention with the quick rise and fall of her chest.

"What?" I asked. Too much blood was in my cock, and I was unable to focus on conversation.

"Last time, it didn't really hurt, but it pinched. I was just wondering if it would hurt again."

"Bee?" I asked, momentarily stunned, my hand still on my cock.

"Yeah?"

"When was the last time you did this?" The question made me want to vomit. I knew what Owen did to her, and he paid the ultimate fucking price. But I hadn't really thought about what she'd done while I was gone. Imagining anyone else touching her was enough to make my dick turn into an innie, but I couldn't blame her. It was my fault. I'd left her on her own. Of course she would've dated, leaned on someone else for comfort.

I was going to fucking puke.

"Four years ago, at the apartment at your shop."

I didn't know exactly what to say, but when I opened my mouth the only thing that came out was "Why, baby?"

"I'd already found you. I wasn't looking for anyone else. You touching me may not burn me anymore." She looked as if what she was saying pained her. "But just the thought of anyone else touching me is still enough to set my skin on fire." Bee's eyes started to water and my heart constricted in my chest.

This girl.

This girl was going to kill me with fucking emotions.

"Only me?" My male pride swelled right along with my cock.

"Only you. It's only ever been you," Bee said, cupping my face in her hands.

I lost it. Opening my mouth to hers, our tongues danced and mingled. Her lips were soft and perfect. I kept imagining how they would look while tonguing my cock, but there would be time for that. Right then, I needed to make her mine again. With little to no control left, I managed to reign it in to reassure Bee that it would be okay. Pulling back from our kiss, I whispered, "I'll go slow. I'll be gentle."

I assured her while completely unsure if I could actually follow through with that promise.

Gentle wasn't my thing.

My dick ached, and all I could think about was sinking into her tight heat.

"No," Bee said.

"No?" I asked.

"No, don't be gentle. Just be mine."

I didn't wait for any more of a confirmation after that, not wanting to give her time to change her mind. I lined my cock up with her entrance, rubbing the head through her wet folds a few times before looking into the glazed over eyes of the woman I loved and sinking my cock deep inside her with one long overdue thrust.

Warm.

Wet.

Soft.

Tight.

Home.

I almost came right then and there. From the sounds Bee was making, I knew she was right there with me. I sat up on the bed and grabbed the back of Bee's neck, dragging her up with me. As I thrust up into her pussy, I looked into her heavily lidded eyes, licked her throat, and grabbed fistfuls of her ass. Stroking her clit with my thumb, I brought her to orgasm for the second time, grabbing her chin to stop her head from falling backward. I needed to look into the eyes of the woman I loved when she came for me, her wetness dripping down to my balls as her pussy clenched around my shaft.

Fucking beautiful.

This woman, with scars inside and out, had chosen *me* to be with. Fucked up, undeserving *me.*

The sick thing was that she knew exactly who I was.

She still wanted me.

She LOVED me.

What the fuck was wrong with her?

I couldn't wait to come any longer. I forcefully pressed Bee back down into the mattress, pummeling her pussy with my cock.

Her pink lips parted, her head thrown back in ecstasy. I was totally mesmerized by the look on her face when my orgasm hit me with wrecking ball type force that could take down a damn building. My balls tightened to the point of pain, my cock spurting streams of hot cum into the pussy it was made to come into.

Holy. Fuck.

I fell back onto the pillows and maneuvered Bee so that she was lying on top of my chest. When I could focus again, I slowly ran my hand through her beautiful red hair. It was the first thing I'd noticed about her. I traced the intricate tattoo on her shoulder with my fingers, slowly making my way around the scars that decorated her back and right arm.

Those scars kept her from connecting with people for so long, but when it came to me, she'd knocked down every barrier she'd ever built so she could let me in.

Into her life.

Into her heart.

Into her body.

My fucking girl. The pride in my heart was almost too much. I squeezed Bee and kissed the top of her head.

"I fucking love you, Bee."

"I fucking love you, too, Jake."

TWO

"Is now a bad time to tell you we should've used a condom?"

"Why? You got the clap?" I teased. Bee's little giggle lit up my dark soul.

"No, but I'm not on anything," She said. Oddly enough, this time around the thought never occurred to me to use protection. This was my woman. I had no plans of ever wrapping it up again. We needed to be as close as possible, skin to skin, and whatever happens, happens. Georgia was by far the greatest gift in the world. An amazing little girl that a bastard like me didn't deserve. I wouldn't mind another just like her, especially since this time I would be able to see Bee with a big baby belly, her tits soft and swollen.

I was getting hard again.

"I figure I would get you barefoot and pregnant as soon as possible anyway. You wouldn't understand. It's a man thing," I joked.

"Oh yeah? So that's your new goal? To knock me up, again?" she asked.

"No, if that happens, it happens. That would be great, but my new goal is actually something else." My stomach had fucking butterflies in it as I prepared to say what I'd wanted to say for so fucking long.

I'm such a motherfucking pussy.

"Oh yeah?" Bee yawned, stretching her arm out over my chest. "What's that?"

I never expected to feel the way I felt about Bee. I never expected to love anyone so completely. She made me feel like at least a part of me was capable of some sort of normal, and since I was able to experience such great love, maybe I wasn't such a monster after all.

Maybe.

Probably not.

"Marry me," I whispered.

Bee froze. I didn't know if she had faded into a sudden deep sleep or was holding her breath. She had about one more second to answer before I shook her awake and demanded a response. It seemed like an eternity before she lifted her head from my chest. The most amazing pair of blue eyes, the eyes I fell in love with four years ago, gazed up at me like I'd hung the fucking moon.

"Okay," she said simply. A tear rolled down her cheek. Her perfect pink lips formed a huge smile meant only for me.

I loved the shit out of this girl.

I reached down and lifted her up on top of me until we were eye to eye. "Okay," I said, pushing her hair behind her ear, then covering her mouth with my own in a deep all encompassing kiss.

The need to be inside her again took hold, my cock harder than the first time around. Rolling over on top of her, she eagerly spread her legs for me. I entered her easily and completely, sheathing myself to the hilt. She took all of me, but gave me even more.

She always had.

I planned on making up for lost time all night.

And then forever.

THREE

One year later...

Reggie and I were at the shop working on our new pet project, restoring an old Shelby Mustang that some kid had blasphemously turned into a fucking donk. A hydraulic system was hooked to the suspension so the car would hop up and down on the tires, the body was painted a matte black from a fucking spray can, and when Reggie pulled it into the lot of my shop and put it in park, the twenty inch gold rims continued to spin. The six inch lift made it almost as tall as my truck.

I imagine that when I died someday, the hell that was waiting for me looked very much like the purple velvet ridiculousness that covered the entire interior.

My stomach rolled when I thought back to the condition it'd been in when I first saw it. Reggie felt the same way because when the kid who was driving it pulled into the parking lot of Bert's Bar one night, Reggie had flagged him down and offered him way more than what it was worth. Thank fucking god the stupid kid accepted his offer, handing over his keys as soon as I rode in with the cash.

I wasn't even mad that Reggie made the deal without asking me first. I'd gladly have paid twice that amount for the opportunity to turn it back into what both God and Ford had intended.

Maybe not necessarily in that order.

I'm glad Abby and Georgia weren't there when the Sheriff showed up that day, fish-tailing his old patrol car into my gravel parking lot like he was a fucking stunt driver for Dukes of Hazard, dust and dirt billowing from under his tires as he skidded to a stop, lights and sirens blaring in the middle of the fucking day. The Sheriff's only deputy followed closely behind him with the only other patrol car in Coral Pines.

Sheriff Fletcher and Deputy Harbord got out of their cars and drew their guns, shielding themselves behind the open doors of their vehicles.

"Get your fucking hands up!" the sheriff ordered through a small portable bull-horn that muffled his voice as if he was repeating our order back to us from the old drive through of the Dairy Queen.

Reggie's hands shot up in the air. "Drop the wrench!" Deputy Harbord shouted.

Reggie looked up to his raised hands and dropped the wrench as soon as he realized he was still holding it. It bounced off the concrete and clattered down into the oil bay.

I lifted my head out from under the hood of the Shelby and wiped my hands with the rag I kept over my shoulder. I took in the scene in front of me as I lit a cigarette and wondered which of my arrestable offenses could've warranted such theatrics.

"To what do I owe the pleasure?" I asked sarcastically. Leaning up against one of the tall tool boxes that lined the outside of the work bay, crossing my legs at the ankles. I took a long drag of my cigarette and blew the smoke out of my nose.

Sheriff Fletcher was as crooked as they'd come. After I

found out he'd helped Owen when he'd raped and almost killed Abby, the motherfucker was lucky he was still fucking breathing.

I couldn't kill everyone.

At least, that's what Abby kept telling me.

"Jacob Francis Dunn?" the deputy asked, slowly approaching the work bay. Sheriff Fletcher stood his ground by his car, gun at the ready.

Fucking coward.

"Griff, put that thing down," I said, gesturing with my cigarette to the gun he had aimed at my chest. "You know me. Don't pretend like you fucking don't." I put out my cigarette on the heel of my boot. "You've know me since the ninth grade when I fingered your girlfriend in the back of the room during English Lit while you gave that presentation on Jane Austen." Griff's face dropped. "Don't worry though. I only made her come once."

"Not exactly the thing to say to someone holding a gun to your head," Griffin spat, his face turned red with irritation. "And it was Shakespeare, asshole."

"So you do remember. It was so long ago, man. You remember the name of that whore you used to date?" I goaded. I already knew the answer.

"Kristy, her name was and is Kristy. And if you say one more word about my fucking wife I'm going to squeeze this here trigger," he warned. "Now put your fucking hands up." He redirected his gun from my chest to my head.

"Everything all right over there?" Sheriff Fletcher called out, still hiding behind his car door.

"I got this, Boss." Griff called back without taking his eyes off me.

"What exactly do you fuckers want?" I asked, irritated that they'd interrupted me while I was resuscitating the Shelby. I'd just started Mustang CPR on her when they'd pulled in.

"Jacob Dunn, we have a warrant for your arrest. We came to take you on in," Griff said, proudly.

"You gonna arrest me?" I asked. "What the fuck for?"

Griff reached behind his back with the hand that didn't have a finger on the trigger and produced a pair of handcuffs from his back pocket. Just about then I noticed that the good sheriff was no longer hiding by his patrol car. Then, I was slammed into from the side, and my chest smashed up against the hood of the Shelby. Cold metal cuffs were slapped tightly around my wrists.

"What am I being charged with?" I asked again as they both yanked me up to my feet, shoving me toward the cars. Sheriff Fletcher planted his hand firmly on the chain connecting the cuffs. "You are under arrest for the murder of Owen Fletcher," He finally answered, before leaning into my ear and whispering so only I could hear. "You messed with the wrong fucking family, boy." His breath hot on my neck, I fought to contain my gag reflex. There was no way I was going to let that fucker know he'd gotten to me in any way, and that included cringing because of his hot garbage breath.

At that moment, Bee pulled her truck into the lot. When she saw what was happening, she jumped down from the drivers seat, leaving the door wide open, the engine still running.

"Jake!" she yelled, her little legs blurring together as she sprinted across the lot.

I planted my feet in the dirt and locked up my knees in an

attempt to hold my ground so I could talk to my wife, but the sheriff pushed on the cuffs and I had to again move forward so I wouldn't wind up face first in the dirt.

"Baby, call a lawyer," I told Bee when she came running up, the idiot lawmen pushing me right passed her.

"Jake! No!" Abby shouted. I was shoved onto the sticky back seat of a patrol car.

"You're gonna need more than a lawyer, boy," Sheriff Fletcher said, slamming the door behind me. He then plopped himself into the driver's seat. "Jesus Christ himself isn't going to get you out of this."

"Lawyer," I mouthed to Abby, who stood with her mouth agape next to the patrol car.

She nodded, crossing her arms protectively over her chest. In what was only the time span of a few short seconds, the look on Bee's face changed from an expression of concern one would expect to see from the wife of a man being dragged away in cuffs, to completely unreadable.

Her eyes glazed over.

Her mouth formed a straight line.

Bee was shutting down.

Fuck no.

No. No. No.

I'll take my girl angry. In fact, I liked getting her riled up from time to time. The way her eyebrows scrunched together when she's trying to yell at me for throwing my smelly fishing shirts in with the regular laundry is fucking adorable, and has resulted in me bending her over the washing machine on more than one occasion.

I'll take my girl sad. I'm a fucked up individual, and for reasons I'll never understand, the taste of her tears made me rock hard. Besides, when Bee was sad, which wasn't often, I could always crack a few inappropriate jokes and make her laugh her way back to happy.

I'll take anything my wife was willing to fucking give me, because the last thing I ever wanted was for Bee to crawl back into that fucking head of hers again and get lost under all the shit she kept buried in there.

At that very moment she was fading away before my eyes, but I needed her to be present, to be strong.

For Georgia.

For our family.

It killed me that I couldn't go to her, hold her in my arms and drag my Abby back to the surface, and, if necessary, I wasn't entirely against shaking the shit out of her until she refocused and emerged from the fog she retreated to when she just couldn't deal.

Dumb and fucking Dumber both drove off the same way they'd arrived. One at a time, tires spinning dramatically in the dirt, launching onto the street, their sirens invading every corner of the usually eerily quiet neighborhood. The wall of mangroves lining the road flashed blue and red as we passed.

Abby stood in the road and watched us drive off, her expressionless face shrinking smaller and smaller in the rearview mirror until she completely disappeared from sight.

I could feel my heart twisting in my chest, and I made a vow right then and there that no matter what happened as a result of these charges, I was going to find my way back to Bee and

Georgia as soon as I could.

Breaking out of prison couldn't be that hard.

We turned toward the Matlacha Pass, the only bridge that connected the rest of the world to Coral Pines. Once we were over the bridge, the sheriff spoke to my reflection in the rearview mirror. "Why is it, Jake, that you don't seem surprised that you are being charged with my nephew's murder?"

I shrugged. "Well, it's been a while since I jaywalked."

The sheriff shook his head. "Touche, Mr. Dunn. Too-fucking-shay," he said, rolling the window down just a crack. He lit a joint he'd retrieved from the center console. "All I'm saying, son, is that I'm hoping they fry your ass real good, hope some skin head with a hankering for blondes makes you his new girlfriend." He held the smoke in his lungs, not even bothering to blow it out the crack in the open window as he finished his little villain speech.

Or was he the good guy, and it was me who was the villain?

The lines between right and wrong, good and bad, light and dark, were always blurred when it came to the comings and goings of the residents of Coral Pines.

You never knew who was going to save you.

Or who was going to kill you.

FOUR

In the back of my mind I always knew that no matter how careful I was, someday there was a possibility the shit I'd done would catch up with me in a very big way.

I knew that day had come when I found myself being led down a poorly lit concrete hallway wearing a scratchy orange jumpsuit, carrying an even scratchier blanket and pillow, into a cell much smaller than the new guest bathroom I'd just finished remodeling for Bee.

Inmates shouted over one another, their voices bouncing off the cement block walls of my cell, any one person indiscernible from the blended echoes of the masses. My eyes watered from the inescapable and overwhelming stench of backed up toilets and body odor.

Although my father had been dead over a year I could almost hear his 'I told you so's' from the grave.

Fuck you, Frank.

My mother, the eternal optimist when it came to me, used to tell me that the world expected great things from me, that my future held something terrific in it, and that someday I would realize my true potential. She usually gave me that speech while she was driving me home from the sheriff's station or from a stint in juvie.

She was sort of right all along. I'd realized my true potential a long time ago. There just wasn't anything terrific about it.

Horrific maybe. *Terrific* no.

I'm not glad she's dead, but I'm glad she would never see me caged up like the monster I was.

My father, Frank, never traveled on the same wavelength of thought my mother did. He always told me that my future held nothing more than a life behind the cold bars of a prison cell. It was laughable, because that drunken fuck might have been actually right for once.

The cell door slammed shut behind me. I set the blanket on the unmade top bunk. The guard locked my cage with one of the many keys on his retractable key chain attached to his belt.

"Welcome home, inmate," he said smugly, tipping up the brim of his baseball cap in mock salute, the cap read CORRECTIONS in big bold gold lettering across the front. The guard, whose brass nametag read ABBOT, sucked on his upper teeth with his tongue as if he'd just finished a big satisfying meal.

I wanted to fucking END him.

I leapt back to the cell door and grabbed a hold of the bars. Abbot gasped in surprise and fell back onto his boney ass. "You spook easy, don't ya, officer?" I growled, squatting down so we were eye to eye. His beady little eyes turned to black, the fear had caused his pupils to dilate.

I was very familiar with that look.

It was a look I quite enjoyed.

I wanted to do a hell of a lot more than just scare the little fucker. "It's so easy to be a smug little shit from the other side of the bars," I said coldly. "Why don't you come on in here with me, and say that sarcastic shit again?"

Even though Officer Abbot was obviously scared shitless, the truth of the matter was that he had the upper hand. I was securely locked into a windowless cage, and although he may have been on his ass, he was on his ass on the freedom side of the bars.

"Maybe I will, inmate." Abbot stood and brushed himself off. The cockiness in his tone wavered. Pointing at me with his nightstick, Abbot looked around to make sure no one had witnessed him almost pissing himself on the floor. "I'm watching you, inmate." He warned. "In here you an't nothin' more than a fucking number. You ain't even worthy of the name your mama gave ya, so if you choose act like a fucking animal, you're gonna be treated like a fucking animal."

With a final bucktoothed sneer, he walked off, dragging his night stick across the bars of my cell, then across all the other cells in the corridor, as he made his way to the only door at the end of the cell block. The inmates shouted obscenities at him as he passed without any sort of reaction from the guard. He signaled to another guard who sat on the other side of a glass partition. The red blinking light above the door temporarily turned green as he was buzzed through, disappearing from site, the door closed with a heavy click, the light above the door once again blinked red.

"Motherfucker," I mumbled, taking a long hard look at my new accommodations. I knew that doing what I'd done for as long as I'd done it, that I was possibly paving a path for myself that lead me right to a cell just like the one I found myself in.

In all honesty, it's a path I never truly thought I would ever be traveling.

If I had to bet money on how my life would end up, with either my early death, long before old age took hold, or a life behind bars, I would've placed my money on death every fucking time.

The DA, some nitwit named Sparrow, was seeking the death penalty, so I guess there was still time to win that bet after all.

I could die tomorrow, and it wouldn't mean jack shit to me. Death was one of the only certainties in this life. It's always been a comfort to me, knowing that since the moment we all first came into this world kicking and screaming, that we were all heading toward the same end.

Although once dead, some people would go in one direction while others, like me, will go in another.

Some of us still kicking and screaming.

The only thing that bothered me about the possibility of dying, was that I wouldn't be around to protect those I vowed to provide for and keep safe. That the time I'd spent with the only two people I didn't feel indifferent about was entirely too short.

Abby. Georgia. My wife. My daughter.

Team redhead as Georgia called them.

My family.

Over the past year, my life seemed like a dream. A dream someone like me was unworthy of even having. Every day of my life was a gift I knew I didn't deserve but selfishly accepted anyway.

Being thrown into a cell was a harsh reminder that life could be both a horrible nightmare and a terrific dream. But they both had something in common.

Eventually, no matter the dream, you always woke up.

FIVE

I'd been in my cell for less than a day, staring at the fucking wall when yet another correctional officer rapped on the bars of my cell with his night stick. "Let's go, let's go!" he shouted impatiently.

"What's with you guys and that shit?" I asked, rubbing my temples. Jail had seeped into my head and started giving me a migraine.

He ignored me. "Let's go, inmate." He unlocked my cell and produced a pair of handcuffs. "Turn around. You have a visitor."

The guard scuffed me, shoving me into a large bright room filled with circular tables. He left me at the door, and I was left to find my visitor on my own.

Inmates, decked out in the same orange prison attire I was sporting, sat next to or across from visitors and people who were very obviously lawyers. At a table in the far corner a woman sat crying, holding the hand of an inmate with a spider web tattoo on the back of his neck while an excited toddler with dark curls ran around the table screaming like he was in Disney instead of a prison. A couple at another table argued, the woman pointing at the man accusingly with a long curved fingernail, the inmate she was visiting appeared disinterested in whatever she was chastising him for.

I knew where Bee would be before I spotted her. I shifted between the tables and made my way to a quiet corner in the back of the room, the one most shadowed by the trees outside the high window. Bee was perched on one of the round stools attached to the table, her back against the wall, hugging her knees to her chest, chewing on her thumbnail, staring out into space.

Bee was always a little awkward when she was uncomfortable, in an adorable, didn't know what to do with her hands, kind of way.

It wasn't what she was doing that surprised me.

It was what she was wearing.

A fucking black hoodie.

Zipped all the way up to her fucking throat.

Just looking at her wearing that thing brought up fond memories of when we first met, and broke my fucking heart at the same time.

She was retreating internally, and I was already forming an idea on how to pull her back out.

I just had to get out of that shit-hole prison first.

Bee's red hair was well past her shoulder blades on the way to her waist, and unlike Georgia's adorable yet unruly curls, Bee's hair was naturally stick straight. She still didn't wear any makeup, her insanely big blue eyes and spattering of freckles were more than enough to dress up her already perfect pale skin and naturally full pink lips.

A year had passed so quickly, just a tiny blip on the radar of the length of time I really wanted to spend with Bee and Georgia. We were just getting started on the forever I'd promised them.

I couldn't lose it all now.

I couldn't lose her.

Ever.

Bee deserved better than me, but I was drawn to her innocence, and she was drawn to my darkness. Together, we made a whole lot of no sense, and it was just the way I liked it.

Lightning striking is too cliché for the moment Abby Ford appeared out of nowhere and literally fell into my life. It felt more like she had me on my knees with a knife to my throat and had me begging for my life, but a new kind of life. One with her in it.

A life worth living.

A person worth living for.

Every day I spend with Bee is another day she breaks my fucking heart and repairs it all over again. Being with her makes the tiny hairs on my arm stand on end and my heart drop into my stomach every time she enters the fucking room.

I LOVED her. I was OBSESSED with her.

If anyone tried to tell me a story that involved love at first sight, I would shake my head and call it a bunch of horseshit. Love in general was a sketchy concept. Instant love was just fucking ridiculous.

Until her.

The only thing with a stronger pull than the monstrous

need to take the life of another was the pull of Abigail Ford.

She didn't show me that I was capable of love. She was the one who made me capable of love.

Of loving her.

Of loving Georgia.

The need for Abby was stronger than my need for anything else.

I loved her.

I still love her.

I will *always* fucking love her.

"Hey," She said. "You okay?"

I couldn't help but laugh.

"Am *I* okay?" There I was worried about her and Georgia and how I was going to protect them from inside a jail cell, and my girl, who was free to be out in the world, was asking *me*, her 6'1" deranged husband with a penchant for dancing with the devil, if *I* was okay.

"Yes," she said, answering my question, but not reacting to my outburst. Normally, Bee would have crossed her arms over her chest and asked me what the fuck I thought was so fucking funny.

"Baby girl." Kneeling in front of her, I took her hands in mine, resting them both on her lap. "I'm laughing because it's a fucking ridiculous question and because you don't ever need to be worrying about me." I pushed a stray hair off of her forehead and tucked it behind her ear. Bee's chin fell to her chest, she took a deep breath. "I'm just fine, baby," I assured her. I pulled her close and pressed my lips to hers. I wished that somehow that kiss would stop whatever thoughts were making her withdraw and snap her out of the place she went to when all wasn't right in her world.

It was a flat out lie, I wasn't okay by any means, but I didn't need Bee worrying about me. The more she worried, the more she would retreat from me and the harder it would be to make things right again. What I wanted to tell her is that without her, without Georgia, even for just a few hours, I was the furthest thing from fine.

But there was no fucking way I was going to tell her that, especially when she was wearing that hoodie. Bee's equivalent of a security blanket. The message she was sending me was loud and clear. She was freaking the fuck out. She was afraid of losing me.

I wasn't afraid of that. She was never ever going to lose me.

I was going to fix this. Fix her. Did she need me to? Probably not, Abby always came out of it on her own with a little time and she was always stronger for it. But this time, this time I was going to be more than her vigilante. This time, when and if I got out of prison, I was going to be her hero.

"No prolonged contact!" A high pitched voice warned. A skinny guard with a red pointed mustache stood by the far wall and glared at us. As much as it pained me, I pulled away from Bee and took a seat next to her, our hands folded together on top of the table, our knees touching underneath. It was the closest I could physically get to her, and I was going to savor every minute of PG contact that I could.

"Your lawyer should be here tomorrow morning," Abby said, reminding me of why we were in that room in the first place. "Have they told you what they have against you? What the evidence is?"

I told Abby what I knew. Which wasn't much. The DA had put me in one of those windowless rooms meant to intimidate, and tried his best to get me to confess, until he realized the only answer I had to any of the questions he'd asked, including if I wanted some coffee, was "I'm not talking without my fucking lawyer." Finally, he'd thrown his arms up in frustration, grabbed his jacket from the back of the chair, knocking it over in the process, and left the room, slamming the door behind him and told them to process me. Next thing I knew, I was in a van and headed north to the jail in Logan's Beach.

What I did learn during his failed interrogation was that the evidence they had against me was enough to charge me with murder in the first degree.

Enough to seek the death penalty.

I didn't mention that to Abby.

"Why are you wearing that again?" I asked her, gesturing to the hoodie.

"It was cold," she said meekly, looking everywhere but at me.

"Hey," I said, turning her chin to me, forcing her to look me in the eyes. "It's okay that you need to be comforted right now. It's okay to feel shitty about this entire situation because it is a shitty situation." I rubbed the pad of my thumb over her cheek. "But it's not okay to check out on me, Abigail Ford. You can't leave me. Ever."

"I'm not..." she started.

I interrupted, "The only thing I like about that hoodie is how it reminds me of how we met. Do you remember that night,

Bee?"

"Yes," she whispered.

"I loved you then."

"No, you didn't." Her eyes turned glassy. I was getting to her so I kept going.

"Yes, I did. I loved you that very night, and I've loved you every single night since, baby." I wiped the tear that fell from the corner of her eye, she leaned into my touch.

It wasn't much, but reminding her of how we got our start was the only thing I could do to help her stay present while I was locked away.

I was making a list of all the shit I was going to do once I was free because my number one priority was going to be making sure my wife knew that I was there to carry her burdens for her and make sure that the life I gave her was one she never felt like she couldn't deal with.

When I got out, Abby and I were going to have a couples' therapy session.

Jake Fucking Dunn style.

SIX

Being locked up gives you only one thing: time to think.

And since Abby's visit, the only thing on my mind was how remembering the night we met had made her tear up. A huge victory when it came to the fragile emotional state of my wife.

She was both the most vulnerable and the strongest person I knew. My very own living breathing oxymoron.

I knew I would get her to react when I brought up the night we met because my own reaction was always strong when I thought about that night.

The night I almost put a bullet in her head.

More felony than fairy tale.

But it still made me smile every time I recalled the first moment my eyes landed on the little ball of attitude who would eventually become my wife.

My world.

I was getting my cock sucked by some girl I went to high school with whose name I barely remembered then or now. I didn't want to bring her into my little apartment attached to the shop because I didn't want her to get the wrong idea and think that what we were doing involved a sleep over.

Or a bed.

Or more than ten minutes.

After I picked the girl up from the Bert's, I drove to my dad's shop and led her out back to the car graveyard. Before I could fully unzip, she'd already thrown her purse onto the asphalt to use as a makeshift cushion and dropped to her knees.

My back was against an old dusty truck, and the chick with my cock down her throat was going at me like I was her last fucking meal. I heard a rustle, but it wasn't enough to distract me from the girl working me with her mouth like it was her fucking job.

Then, there was a sneeze. I will never forget that sneeze for as long as I live. It seemed to come from nowhere.

The girl I was face-fucking didn't seem to notice.

It sounded really close.

Too fucking close.

The girl deep-throated my cock, pulling me in further than I thought possible. Before I could form another coherent thought, I was coming, and she was punching my my thighs with closed fists and spitting onto the pavement, screeching at me for not warning her I was about to come. I laughed because I grew up in Coral Pines, and there wasn't a guy I knew that hadn't shot his load in her throat before tenth grade. She stomped to the fence, and I followed her to let her out, sliding the gate shut behind her. She walked away mumbling to herself, but I was to preoccupied with the sneeze to give a fuck about what she was bitching about.

I took off my jacket and set it on a bicycle with no seat.

Slowly, I crept back to the old truck and pulled my gun from the waistband of my jeans. It was when I rounded the truck that I first saw a ball of black hoodie hunched over on his knees. Whoever it was had puked onto the pavement.

I aimed my gun at his head and cocked it. The hoodie froze.

"Who sent you, motherfucker?" I asked. Stepping forward, I pressed the barrel of my gun against his head.

No answer.

"So you want to play it that way, huh?" I asked angrily. I grabbed at the hoodie, yanking it back over the intruders face. I was glad that I was going to be able to hand down my own brand of perverse justice on this guy.

I was already planning his disposal when I was suddenly distracted by something soft in my hand. It was a clump of long, bright red hair.

What the fuck?

I looked from my hand to the small figure crumpled in front of me. I nudged him in the back of the head with the barrel of my gun. He finally turned and looked up.

SHE looked up.

Huge innocent blue eyes masked in pale skin stared up at me. Not a woman. A girl, no older than seventeen or eighteen.

A beautiful girl.

THE most beautiful girl.

My girl.

I was twenty-two. Not an old man by any means, but too old for a girl as young as her. It was wrong for me to be drawn to her the way I was. But my brain, my dick, and my thawing heart didn't seem to give a flying fuck about propriety.

It sounds so fucking cliché, but it was when our eyes first met when my life changed irrevocably.

I wouldn't say that I believe in any sort of destiny, but if something like that did exist, it was working that night. Abby crossing my path was when my life took another path the fork in the road of life offered, and I'd never looked back.

Although it wouldn't be an easy road traveled by any means, the scared girl on her knees before me would eventually welcome me into her life, into her body.

She would bear my child.

She would become my wife.

That skinny girl with the oversized sweat shirt had suffered so much in her life and little did either of us know then that she would suffer so much more.

Fucking OWEN.

The mere mention of his name was enough to send me into a rage right there in the visiting area.

It wasn't until Abby finally told me what Owen did to her, when she showed me the pictures, the evidence of a crime that makes my stomach roll every time I fucking think about it, when I'd learned that the true depths of my sickness and depravity had no limits when it came to protecting both Abby and Georgia.

Vengeance was a drug I main-lined the night I tracked down that bastard. Revenge was the high I rode when I removed him from this fucking earth.

Love is what made it all make sense. When it came to my girls and my love for them, any rules I had about how and why I do the things I do were thrown out the window.

Our love had no rules.

What I did to Owen made me realize that there was a reason I was put on the planet exactly how I was, how I am.

To protect my family.

SEVEN

The meeting with my lawyer went as well as could be expected for someone being charged with first-degree murder.

Henry Allbright, one of the only competent lawyers within ten miles of Coral Pines, had informed me that there was a witness to the crime.

Of sorts.

A gator.

A mother fucking alligator.

All these years doing god knows what to god knows fucking who and I was going down partially because a fucking lizard had to go and get caught before it had the chance to properly digest its midnight snack of Owen Fletcher parts.

The guy who'd caught it was quite surprised to find a hand minus a few fingers in the belly of the beast he was gutting.

Impressive feat for the gator.

Damning for me.

The surveillance footage from the marina cameras across the street from the boathouse where I'd caught up to Owen, showed him entering the building, then me following him in shortly after.

But that wasn't the damning part.

The damning part was me, emerging hours later.

Two black garbage blanks slung over my back.

The camera never picked up Owen leaving, but what it did pick up was the license plate on my bike.

After the FBI identified Owen from his dental records and learned he'd shot my daughter just a few days before his 'alleged' (their words, not mine) death, they had a clear motive along with enough evidence, albeit circumstantial, to end me.

They had half of Coral Pines lined up as witnesses ready to testify that Owen and I had our share of public scuffles in the past.

The case was wrapped up neat and tied in a mother fucking bow, they had me by the balls.

The judge denied bail.

The question was, if they had all this evidence for a year, why did it take them so long to arrest me? Why would they sit on this for so long before making their move?

This wasn't the Coral Pines Sheriff's Department stumbling their way through an investigation. This was the motherfucking FBI. There was no reason for the delay in my arrest that made any sort of sense to me and that wasn't the only thought keeping me up at night.

I couldn't sleep in jail. I hadn't slept a single night without Bee for over a year and was beginning to wonder if I was ever going to be able to sleep again.

Just a few nights earlier, I was fast asleep in the king sized bed I shared with my wife. My arms wrapped tightly around her, not an inch between us as I held her tightly to my chest. Her steady breathing was a constant reminder that she was there with me and wasn't going anywhere.

A shift on the mattress woke me, and I instantly sat up straight on full alert, only to find my daughter slowly crawling up from the foot of the bed.

"What's the matter, baby?" I'd asked, making space so Georgia could snuggle between me and Abby. Abby turned over onto her side, but didn't wake up.

"I dreamed bad dreams, Daddy," Georgia said, rubbing her eyes, her stuffed rabbit in the crook of her arm. I pulled the covers over us and she rested her head against my chest.

"They're only dreams, Gee. Daddy would never let anything or anyone ever hurt you," I said, brushing the curls from her eyes.

"Pinky promise?" she whispered, extending her pinky to me.

"Pinky promise," I repeated, hooking my pinky with hers. And I meant it. There was no way I was ever going to let anything happen to my little girl. My fighter. My survivor.

When Bee and I had sex for the very first time, I'd used a condom, but I was so wrapped up in Abby that I'd fallen asleep inside her, afraid to pull out like she would disappear if I did, rendering that little piece of rubber virtually useless.

It's the only time in my life I could look back on and be thankful for my stupidity.

Georgia was in the first moments of creation when Abby was brutalized by Owen, but somehow, through all that violence, our daughter had held on tight and didn't let go.

She grew big and strong inside my wife.

Abby says Georgia was born with a set of lungs that would scare the devil straight.

How appropriate.

Even though I didn't meet her until she was three years old, for the second time in my life, it was love at first sight.

I'd thought Georgia was Owen's daughter at first, the product of a relationship between him and Bee, but I still loved her, wanted her to be mine.

Wanted her to love me back.

I would walk to the ends of the earth for Abby.

I would burn the motherfucker down for Georgia.

In prison, if the mattress dipped in the dead of night, it definitely wasn't because your sweet baby girl was wanting some cuddles with you. But I wasn't afraid of the other inmates trying to come at me. The only stabbing I was afraid of receiving would come at the hands of the loose springs of the stained mattress I attempted to sleep on.

Every hour on the hour the guards made their rounds, shining their flashlights into the faces of the sleeping inmates, making sure each one was accounted for. The squeak of the guards' boots against the concrete floor for the umpteenth time during the night wasn't a surprise.

My cell door being unlocked and opened was. I pretended to be asleep, preparing myself to defend my honor against whatever fucker had a fetish for blondes with tattoos.

"I know who you are," A voice said. A lighter ignited, from the corner of my half closed eye I saw the cherry end of a cigarette burning a few feet from my bed. Whoever it was sat on the floor with his back against the concrete wall.

"And who exactly do you think I am?" I asked, calculating how to take him out if he made a move.

"A mutual friend of ours calls you The Moordenaar."

The fucking Dutchman, the man who gave me my first job, and the first and only one of my employers to ever know my real identity. The Moordenaar, a Dutch word for 'murderer', is what he called me.

Subtle.

I should slit The Dutchman's throat for not being able to keep his fucking mouth shut. Fuck it. I'll add it to my list of shit to do when I got out. "Wrong guy," I said, turning to look at the guy invading my personal space.

Small yellow lights lining the walkway outside my cell and the light from the half-moon through a high window on the far side of the cell block was all the light I needed to make out that the guy in my cell was huge. A wall of muscle sat on the ground a few feet from my bed, a cigarette hung from his lip, black and white tattoos covered the backs of his hands and one side of his neck, his dark hair cropped close to his head.

His eyes were black and in the light of the half moon he

looked like a man possessed.

I may have been the devil, but with my blonde hair and blue eyes I know I didn't look the part. This guy looked like the floor had opened up and he'd just stepped through the gates of hell and into my cell.

"What do you want?" I asked.

"I need your help." He never took his eyes off of me.

"I don't know you. Why would I help you?" I swung my legs over the side of the bed and sat up.

"You killed the guy who hurt your family, am I right?" he asked.

"Allegedly," I reminded him. I wasn't about to admit anything to this guy. For all I knew, he was working for the DA and wearing a wire.

He laughed and shook his head. "I understand why you would say that, but I'm coming to you because I'm out of options."

"I'm semi-retired," I admitted.

"Well, Jake, I need you to semi-unretire, because my girl is in trouble and there are people that need to be killed."

This guy wasn't fucking around.

"Even if I wanted to help you, I can't do shit from in here and I'm not getting out anytime soon," I told him.

"You'll be out." He stood up, then lightly rapped on the bars. Seconds later, a guard appeared and opened my cell to let him back out. "And I'll be in touch."

When he was long out of sight, I realized I hadn't even

gotten his name.

What the fuck had just happened?

EIGHT

When the guard came to get me from my cell, I figured that I was on my way to meet with my lawyer to work out some sort of defense strategy. When we passed by Visitation and went into a room where they handed me the clothes I was wearing when they processed me, I was utterly confused. I didn't say anything just in case it would make them realize their mistake and I was led back to my cell.

When I took my first step of freedom outside the gates of the jail, the bright light of day blinded me after spending so much time in a dark cell.

The first person I saw was Bethany, who honked the horn of her car and waved me over. "Get in," she ordered, leaning over to open the passenger seat of her SUV.

I got in and waited until we were on the main road before I said anything.

"Why am I out?" I asked. "Where's Abby?" I should have been happy, but my frustrations got the best of me. "Bethany, what in the fuck is going on?"

"The DA dropped the charges, and Abby is at home with Georgia," she said casually, shrugging her shoulders, then adjusting the air conditioning vents.

"Why would they do that? How can they go from not

setting bail to releasing me in less than 72 hours?" I was free, but I was on edge. Something wasn't right.

"Let's just say their witnesses weren't as reliable as they initially thought. In a case that is circumstantial at best, it's the witnesses that make or break it." She looked straight ahead at the road in front of us. She didn't make any sort of eye contact with me but adjusted the rearview mirror for the third time.

"What did you do?" I asked her. There was no way she didn't have a hand in my release.

A small, sly, corner of the mouth smile. A little glimpse at the pit bull lawyer Bethany used to be before morphing herself into a grandmother figure for Georgia. The woman who would move heaven and hell to win a case and who would do anything it took to win a case.

ANYTHING.

There was no doubt in my mind that she did something to cause those witnesses to become 'unreliable'.

"It was the oddest thing, really," Bethany said. "All of the witnesses who were going to testify that you and Owen were mortal enemies suddenly remembered what great friends you two were, how much time you spent together, how much you loved and respected one another. And then there was the little matter of your wedding." Bethany's smile was now a full toothed grin.

"Our wedding?"

"Yes, your wedding. It's odd that it had slipped their minds that they attended your wedding reception and that Owen was your best man."

"My best man?"

"Yes, you see since Owen was the best man at your wedding, which took place at Bert's Bar weeks after his alleged death, there was no way he could be dead, right? There was also the fact that he signed your marriage license as a witness which was filed by the court and a matter of public record..."

"Bethany..." I started, unsure of exactly what to ask her next.

"And of course, as Owen's mother I told the FBI that he disappeared often, sometimes for months on end and that I'd heard from him recently."

"Say what?"

"Yes, I told them that I'd heard from him recently, and he told me about an accident he'd had with his hand while gator hunting. He was still distraught about accidentally hurting Georgia when he was tinkering with his old shot gun, so he didn't have any plans to come back to town just yet."

And there she was, Bethany, the most ruthless grandmother in Coral Pines.

"Why did they wait so long to charge me if they had all these things in place a year ago?"

"Owen's father. He wasn't buying the story that Owen just took off, mostly because Owen had stopped using his credit cards the night he went missing, so when they discovered the hand and the surveillance video he used all his leverage with the DA to push everything forward even though the case was shady at best. Took him a while, but that persistent bastard wouldn't take no for an answer."

"How do you know he isn't still going to try and take me down somehow?" I couldn't relax until I knew I was out for good. That I could hold my family and not be worried about being dragged back in again.

"Because, Jake, he may have been a lousy husband, but he's a very smart man. I told him if he continued down this path that I would cop to Owen's murder myself, and since the bastard won't even sign the divorce papers because he's afraid of how it would look, he wasn't about to let me go down for murdering our son."

"How, how did you get the witnesses to change their stories?" I wasn't close enough to anyone to have them lie for me because they liked me.

Bethany thought for a moment. "You see Jake, the secrets of Coral Pines run deep. Like roots from an old tree, they grow and grow. For years, they spread under the surface until the roots are too big, and the surface starts to crack."

"What does that have to do with the witnesses?"

"Because, Jake, I'd been in Coral Pines long enough to know when it was time to do a little digging under the surface."

"So, basically, you blackmailed them using shit you had against them?"

"Blackmail is such an ugly word." Bethany patted my knee. "I just pulled up some roots."

NINE

Abby

The last thing in this world I ever wanted was for my daughter to suffer like I had. I spent every single day since the moment I brought her into this world making sure that her childhood looked nothing like the living hell of mine.

That's why at night I waited until after I helped her change into her pajamas, after I read her a bed time story, after I tucked her in and kissed her forehead, after I slowly closed her door and crept down the hall, and after I made my way outside to the patio, to sob uncontrollably into my hands.

Georgia had scars.

Lots of scars.

Some deeper than mine.

Scars from the bullet spray, scars from the multiple surgeries to remove what shrapnel they could. Scars resembling white and red paint splatter across her ribcage from armpit to waist on her left side.

I'd failed her, I'd failed my baby girl, and now she was going to have to live with the exact same fate I never wanted for her.

All this on top of Jake being arrested for Owen's murder, and I was again seeking solace in my old hoodie. I tried to call on the numbness but I couldn't reach the place where I couldn't exist anymore. Georgia and Jake had made it impossible for me to retreat completely, but I was trying, because thinking about Jake being locked a way for life or put to death for that bastard's murder made my stomach twist. Because I'd encouraged him to do it.

It would have all been my fault.

"Baby, not again," Jake said, coming up from behind me, his hand on my shoulder. He knew my reaction every time I saw her scars and where I went to hide my reaction from her.

He'd noticed the change in me. I saw it in the way he was more carful around me, practically walking on egg shells, choosing his words more carefully.

I hated it. But I didn't know how to get back to how I was, and with all that was going on inside of me, I didn't know if I wanted to.

"I can't help it." I wiped the tears from under my eyes and sniffled. "I failed her Jake. She is going to look in the mirror every single day and remember that horrible moment for the rest of her life. She'll remember how scared she was. She'll remember how mommy couldn't stop it from happening to her."

"Bee, she's so young. She sees the head shrinker. He says she will be fine. She barely remembers anything at all, and he thinks that even with a fuck up like me as her father that she is going to be okay," Jake assured me, trying to make me laugh as always.

"Yeah, but what about later? What about when one day if she does remember everything? What then? I don't want her to relive that pain every single day of her life."

"Then we will deal with it, Bee. We make sure she knows how much she is loved and when and if she freaks the fuck out, we will again remind her of how much she is loved, and if it gets worse, we will love her even fucking harder. The only bad thing that is ever going to happen to Georgia again is that she might suffocate under all our love." Jake circled my chair and crouched down in front of me. "It's all we can do," he said softly, his hands on my knees. He tilted my chin up so we were eye to eye. "What's this really about, Bee?"

I sighed. "She deserves better than me as her mom."

"That's a fucking cop out, and you know it. All parents are fucked up. We are just fucked up in a different kind of way. Now spill it, woman," he demanded. "Tell me what is going on in that beautiful red head of yours."

"I still see them." I blurted.

"Still see what?"

"I still see my scars. Every day. Even under all the tattoos, I still see right past the colors and right to the marks. Every single fucking day of my life, I'm reminded of what happened, what that bitch did, and even if it's just for a minute, I remember what it felt like." My eyes started to water, blurring my vision. "I remember the hurt. I feel it all over again. I don't want to feel it anymore."

Jake softly ran his fingertips across the largest scar that started on my shoulder and slowly traced it down to my elbow and back up again. His go-to way to way of comforting me. "I can't imagine how badly it hurt, Bee."

"Not there," I said.

"No?"

"No," I took his hand and placed it over my heart. "Here. It hurts here."

Jake scooped me up like I weighed nothing and sat back down in the chair, arranging me on his lap like an infant, cradling me in his arms and holding me tightly to his chest.

"I don't want your heart to hurt. Tell me what I can do to make it better," Jake said, his voice strained.

"It hurts me that Georgia might feel like this someday."

"Her scars are still healing, baby. We will do whatever it takes to make it so she doesn't hurt. But you can't be worried about what she will or won't feel. We have to take this day by day, or you're going to make yourself crazy."

"I know," I sniffled.

"What can I do to make it better?" He kissed the top of my head.

"I don't know that there is anything you can do. You can't wipe my memories away. You can't make me think of something else when I see the marks. It was so much better for a while. So much easier than it used to be. Then Georgia got hurt, and now it's like I'm right back where I started."

"We, baby. We," Jake said. "You don't have to go through this alone. We're a family, and we will fix this as a family."

"But you can't fix it."

"No, but I can help you," Jake said.

"How?" I whispered.

"Do you trust me?"

"Yes." I didn't even hesitate. Jake is the only person in the world I did trust. He was Georgia's father. He helped me to feel again when I thought I was going to live my life without ever knowing what it was like to be close to anyone. There was no reason NOT to trust him.

"I've been thinking about something. Something that could help. Stay here for a minute," Jake ordered, lightly pushing me off of him. He stood and pulled his cell from his pocket pressing one of the speed dial buttons.

After a few seconds of ringing, I heard someone pick up.

"Bethany," Jake said stoically. Why was he calling Bethany? Usually I was the middleman between Bethany and Jake. They rarely spoke, and it's not like I blame them. Bethany spawned Owen and tried to protect him when she knew what he'd done, but I'd already looked past it. Anytime I feel the anger or resentment toward her that I once felt, I just remember how it felt to set her house on fire, and I'm quickly brought back to feeling that all is right between us.

The new Bethany barely resembled the old one, and

her love for Georgia, the granddaughter she never had, had been a big part of setting things right in my eyes. Bethany had spent the last year proving to our family that she was worthy enough to be a part of it.

"Yup. Yeah. Everything is fine. Georgia is great. Yeah," he said rather rudely. "Can you come and sit with Georgia for a bit? She's asleep, but I need to take the boat out for a spin to make sure it's seaworthy for the morning, and I need Bee to come and be my second eyes and ears." There was a short pause, then Jake ended the call without saying good-bye.

"You know, for someone who can be so charming, you really can be a total twat, sometimes," I said.

"Did you just call me charming?" Jake laughed. Off course, that would be the thing that got his attention, not being called a twat. Even in the dim light of the back porch, Jake's smile was brilliant. Being able to see him smile on a daily basis and or laugh on occasion was worth every single second of time we'd spent apart.

I ignored his question. "If you needed help with the boat, why didn't we just do it earlier?" I asked. We'd had a great day as a family. Jake worked on the boat a bit. Georgia ran through the sprinklers in the back yard, and I sat in my favorite chair on the patio, reading a book, glancing over the pages every so often to make sure my family was still there, and that it was all still real.

And it was.

It was getting late, and it was already dark. It would be hard to check the boat for anything under these conditions.

"Shhhhh, baby. You'll see. You said I couldn't make it better for you. I think there is a way I can," Jake said, pressing a finger over my partially opened mouth. I glared at him and bit the

66

tip of his finger. He pulled back his hand, and his jaw dropped open.

"Oh, Bee," he said, his voice full of warning, or was it promise? "You're gonna pay for that one." Briefly sucking on the tip of the finger I'd just bit.

Bethany arrived within a few minutes of Jake's call. The second he opened the door, she scooted past him into the house.

"Come on in," Jake said sarcastically, closing the door behind her. Bethany had already settled herself on the couch and was riffling through the contents of her tote bag.

"You two get where you need to be. I'm fine here," she said, pulling out two knitting needles and some pink yarn. Whatever project was attached to the needles looked pretty ragged.

"Knitting?" I asked her, gesturing to her hands, and she began to absentmindedly knit. Bethany, the once sharp as a tack, uber powerful lawyer whose claws were almost as sharp as her tongue was sitting on my couch, in my living room, knitting. It was bafflingly out of character for her.

Bethany crossed the needles over one another, her tongue stuck out of the side of her mouth as she concentrated. Her foot tapped along with her knitting pace.

She barely paused to breathe when she spoke. "Well, yeah, since I don't have a job anymore to keep me occupied, I needed something to take up some of my time so I don't die of boredom. My shrink suggested I get a hobby so I went on the iPad, and I watched a few of those YouTube videos, or whatever they are called, you know, the ones where a ten year old with a video camera can basically teach you everything you need to know and make you feel old as dirt at the same time? So here we are, halfway to a sweater for Georgia." Bethany had quit her job as the district attorney shortly after Georgia was hurt. In her words 'her 'right and wrong' radar needed a reset, and she couldn't do that and still be the pit-bull lawyer without a conscious she was paid to be.

Bethany held up the small scrap of something that was connected to the needles, I could see the disappointment on her face through the two big holes in the middle of the patch. She shook her head. "It's a work in progress." She said, starting her knitting again. "Over, under, and through." She muttered as she furrowed her brows and squinted down at her work.

"We'll be back in a little while," I assured her. Not actually sure how long whatever it was Jake had planned would take. "Thanks for coming over on such short notice." Before I turned to go, Bethany looked up from her project, her eyes watery.

Thank you. She mouthed to me, and in a flash, she was again back to knitting. "Take your time. I'll be at this darn thing all night anyway." The impatient biting tone back in her voice.

Jake didn't say good bye to Bethany. He didn't say anything for that matter. He opened the sliding glass doors and ushered me through, following closely behind me. Jake took my hand and led me down the backyard to the dock, and when we got there, he sat me down on a plastic bench that doubled as a storage trunk for all of Georgia's pink fishing gear. I picked up a little pink visor with the words DADDYS LITTLE FISHING GIRL monogramed across the front that had fallen behind the bench. I ran my fingers over the raised lettering and sighed to myself.

We'd come so far in such a short period of time. Georgia and Jake both acted like they'd always been part of each other's lives. Sure, I may have birthed her and fed her and clothed her on my own for years, but then Jake showed up and BOOM.

Daddy's little girl to her very core.

I wouldn't have it any other way.

In my life, I'd never experienced the type of love that exists between a father and daughter. The closest thing I ever had to a father was Jake's dad Frank, and although he would always hold a special place in my heart for all he did for me and Georgia, he was rarely sober enough to show off the fatherly side of himself.

I knew nothing of the love between a parent and child until Georgia came along, and she became my entire world.

Watching Jake with Georgia was always a new experience for me. They wore their love for each other on their sleeves. There was no doubt that when anyone looked at the two of them together that they would see that they were enamored with one another.

I know Jake loved me, and that love was limitless. But I knew that the love he felt for Georgia was on a whole other level.

Jake's fishing boat, a twenty foot outboard that used to belong to his brother, sat up on a lift he'd built to keep barnacles from growing on the hull and the saltwater from eating at the paint, he'd just put a new motor on it.

Jake was taking Georgia out early the next morning for their inaugural fishing trip on the newly fixed boat. Meanwhile I would head out while it was still dark to photograph the sun rising over the beach for my newest set of post cards.

It's funny actually because Georgia had to literally be dragged out of bed on most mornings when the sun was already high in the sky, but when Jake was taking her fishing, her eyes sprang open before the sun had even started to peek over the horizon and was usually the one bouncing on our bed to wake Jake up first.

Jake picked up some sort of netting that was spread out on the grass above the seawall. He wrapped it around his arm a few times and set it in a bucket.

"What's that?" I asked him as he set the bucket down next to the storage bench.

"I'm teaching Gee how to throw the cast net tomorrow. Since she likes fishing so much, it's 'bout time she learned how to catch her own bait," he said, his southern accent had grown thicker since he'd come home to Coral Pines. I sometimes forgot that with all of Jake's inner turmoil, and all the things he was capable of doing, that some part of him was just a southern boy who liked to fish and tinker with trucks.

"That net thing is bigger than she is. How much does it weigh?" I asked, noticing that Jake's very toned bicep muscles strained when he'd lifted the bucket.

"Oh, it's pretty heavy, but that one isn't hers," He said. "This one is." Jake reached behind the bench I was sitting on and grabbed a smaller bucket. He opened it and tilted it toward me so I could see the noticeable smaller net inside.

Of course, it was pink.

My heart broke in the best of ways.

"Duke over at the bait shop is starting to question my sexuality with all this pink fishing shit," Jake said with a smile. "Gonna have to start going to the big chain stores in Logan Beach to dodge the rumor mill."

"Fuck the rumor mill," I said. And I meant it. Anyone who came between Jake and Georgia doing something they loved together would have to answer to me.

"Yeah, fuck them, baby," Jake said, adding the smaller

bucket to the boat. He lifted the panel cover for the electric to the lift and hit the switch to lower the boat into the water. It creaked and groaned, the sound of metal on metal made the hairs on my arm stand on end as the heavy wires that held up the boat slowly uncoiled from the spinning wheel at the top of the lift.

"What exactly are we doing?" I asked.

Jake ignored me and pointed to the back of the boat once it was fully floating on top of the water. "Do you think she'll like it?"

"Of course, you know she loves the boat. You put a lot of hard work into it and..." I stopped myself from saying anything else because I realized that it wasn't the boat he was talking about. It was what was written on the back of the boat. In bold cursive lettering to one side of the motor it simply read 'Gee'.

My throat felt like something was caught in it. "No Jake, she isn't going to like it. She is going to love it and freak out and not be able to stop talking about it for days."

Jake lit a cigarette. He looked pleased with my reaction and with himself. "That's what I was going for. You know it was between that and buying her a pony. I'm not cleaning up horse shit."

Jake smiled and stepped down into the boat, holding out his hand to help me onboard. Jake fired it up, and I took the seat next to his. He turned on the spotlight and backed us out of the dock. We puttered down the canal, the spotlight shining off the eyes of a few alligators, and scattered the iguanas lining the seawall, some of them diving into the water, others found refuge in the mangroves.

The open waters of the Coral Pines River shone orange with the glow of the full moon. Jake pressed down on the throttle, and it felt as if we were skating on top of the calm waters, the warm salty air skipping over the front windshield, tangling in my hair.

With all the ugliness I'd experienced here, it was easy to overlook how beautiful the place really was.

We were only on the open water for a few minutes before Jake slowed the boat in the middle of the river. He pulled to the side of a marker, killing the engine when we were hidden between the mangroves of a small cove. He tossed the anchor.

"Why are we out here, Jake?" I asked. It was so quiet my regular tone of voice sounded like a scream.

"I told you why, baby. I figured out a way to help you." He lit another cigarette, rested his elbows on his knees and leaned toward me. "And this is where I think I should do it," he said so quietly it was almost a whisper.

"Do what?" I whispered back. My heart now firmly in my stomach.

"You trust me, don't you?"

"Why do you keep asking me that?" Yes, of course I trusted him. I would trust him with my life and Georgia's, but it was the second time he'd asked me the same question, and that was making me nervous.

Jake put out his cigarette in an old soda can and stood up, holding out his hands to me. "Come here," he said. Pleading with his eyes.

I stood and took his hands. He pulled me into him and pressed his warm lips to mine. I was so caught up in the kiss that I hadn't noticed the small knife in his hand. He pulled back from our kiss and held up the knife between us.

"What is that for?" I swallowed. My heart beating loud enough for fish to hear.

Jake kissed that magical spot behind my ear and whispered against my neck. "I want to cut you."

"What?" I breathed. His words frightening, his touch tempting. I didn't know which way was up. I didn't think I'd heard him right, because he couldn't have just said that he wanted to cut me.

"You say that you look at your scars every single day, and you remember what happened. You feel the hurt all over again, and as much as I want to, I can't take that away for you, but I can do something else." Jake took a deep breath. I can give you a new mark, a new scar associated with a good memory so that when you see your scars, there will be a tiny bit of good mixed in with all the bad."

There was a reason why I loved Jake, why I was drawn to him from the get-go.

He fucking gets me.

No shrink, no meditation, no standard orthodox method of mental repair was going to fix me, and Jake knew it. So he offered me what he could.

"Do it," I breathed. I hated the idea of being cut, but I loved what he was offering me. The scars had me trapped in my own mind. He was offering me freedom. "Do it."

Jake didn't answer me. He just pulled me into him and kissed me, his tongue seeking entrance. With one hand on the back of my head, he tangled his fingers in my hair and pulled until my head tilted back and I opened my mouth to him. He smelled of sweat and the salt water. He tasted like mint and cigarettes. I couldn't get close enough. He pushed me back until the back of my knees hit the small bench seat in the back of the boat. Jake pulled back from me and unbuttoned my shorts. I lifted my hips to so he could slide them down my thighs. He tossed them on the captain's chair and hooked his thumbs into the waistband of my panties and slid them down. He ran his tongue from my belly button down to my clit softly sucking on my sensitive bud as he tossed my panties overboard.

"Hey!" I tried to argue with him about discarding my underwear, but he just lapped his tongue over me, pulling my legs up over his shoulders as he knelt down in front of me. I quickly forgot what I was about to say.

He licked my core like he was kissing me. It was intimate, soft, yet sexy and passionate. He was telling me he wanted me with his tongue, and my pussy was responding in turn by pulsing around his tongue as he licked and sucked on my folds.

I vaguely remembered him saying something about cutting me, about not replacing the bad memories, but dominating over them. I couldn't focus. The boat was rocking from side to side as I tried to buck my hips. Jake held me in place with his strong hands, pulling me toward him and devouring me with his tongue like I was his last meal.

I opened my eyes as my orgasm hit. Staring up at the night sky, I clenched my thighs around Jake's head as I was pelted by wave after wave of pure fucking pleasure, courtesy of sexy Jake fucking Dunn.

My HUSBAND.

Jake didn't wait for me to come down. He stood, removed his belt, pulled down his jeans and in one swift motion flipped me onto my stomach, I gripped the edge of the boat to brace myself. I felt his knees against my ass and then he was seeking entrance, rubbing himself in my wetness before pushing his way inside. My body stretched to extreme lengths to accommodate his size and when he was fully seated inside my body, I felt so full I thought I was going to burst at the seams.

Jake thrust into me once. Hard. I shrieked in surprise, and my insides clenched around him. He bent over me with his chest over my back and kissed the base of my neck as he pulled out and thrust into me again. Hard.

The buildup was slow at first, but as Jake continued his assault on my sex, it continued to grow and grow until I was pushing my ass back toward him and silently begging for some sort of release. I heard a clicking noise and didn't realize what was happening until my orgasm slammed into me. I was vaguely aware of a sharp scratching sensation running down my arm but I was focusing on the release of the most amazing pressure. Everything inside me was alive and content. Jake grabbed my hips and with every deep thrust he pulled me hard against him. Faster and faster until he pushed in as far as he could, then pulled out. Hot liquid spurted out onto my ass.

A different kind of liquid dripped down my arm.

"Come here, baby," Jake said, pulling me up by my arm, setting me on his lap. Jake pulled out a first aid kit and started cleaning the blood off my arm with an alcohol swab. "Did I hurt you?" Concern written all over his face.

"No," I said honestly.

"Good. Because I think this will do the trick." I looked down at my arm. Next to the deepest scar Jake had followed the lines of my tattoos and carved a line about six inches in length into my skin. Not deep enough to cause permanent damage, but deep enough to leave a mark.

A visible scar.

Now, when I looked at my arm, I would see my scars and remember that one of them held a great memory.

Jake had given that to me.

Jake pulled out a needle and thread, and to my surprise, he started stitching me up.

"How do you know how to do that?" I asked.

"I had to do it to myself a few times."

"Do I want to know more?" I asked.

"Nope."

"Okay then." I cupped his face in my hands and brought his mouth to mine. I pressed my lips against his, trying to convey my gratitude to him with that kiss. "Thank you."

"No need to thank me. You would've done the same."

"Yes, I would have. So please, when you need to be sliced open, let me know. I'm your girl." I laughed at the absurdity of it all.

"Yes, you are my girl," Jake said softly, ignoring my sarcasm. Closing the first aid kit and setting it aside, he returned my kiss. Sucking my bottom lip into his mouth, he ran his tongue across my lips slowly. The passion from earlier sated, his kiss wasn't sexual, it was sensual.

I looked down at the crooked sew job on my new arm wound then back up at Jake.

"I fucking love you," I said.

"I fucking love you too, Bee."

EPILOGUE

Abby

Knock-knock-knock-knock-knock-knock-knock

"Just a minute!" I called out to whomever was at the door.

More frantic knocking.

"Just a freaking minute!" I yelled again, setting my open book on the coffee table, hoping it wouldn't close so I could get right back to where I'd left off. I had a thing about my books, and dog earring the page was out of the fucking question. The clock above the TV said it was after ten. Georgia had long been asleep and Jake was on his way home, he'd stayed at the shop late tinkering on my truck which wasn't running AGAIN. I refused to let him buy me a new one no matter how much he pushed the issue. The truck was all I had left of Nan and I wasn't just about to let it go when I knew Jake could work his magic on it. Although the poor thing might have been telling me that it was time to let her go because it was the third time in a month Jake had to repair or replace something to get it back up running again.

Fucking suicidal truck.

I opened the door and had my hand on the handle of the screen door, about to tell Mrs. Flannagen for the umpteenth time that no matter how many times she stopped by on a Saturday night that Jake and I would not be attending church this Sunday or any Sunday after that, when the door flew open and I was met with a massive wall of man.

Dark and scary as fuck.

Jake was easily six feet tall but this guy had at least a few inches on him. His dark hair was cropped close to his head, his eyes shiny black. Where Jake had tattoos up and down one arm, this guy was covered on both arms and hands and even one side of his neck. Jake's light hair and bright blue eyes made him look like the boy next door, almost angelic in a way.

This guy looked like the fucking devil himself.

I made a move to slam the door shut but his boot in the threshold prevented it from closing, he didn't even flinch when it bounced off his foot.

"I need Jake." The man demanded. His voice deep and raspy.

I reached behind the door and grabbed the pistol from the top drawer of the hallway desk, shielding it behind my back.

"He's not here." I said. I made another move to shut the door but this time he used the flat of his hand to prevent it from shutting.

"You're not fucking listening, I need Jake." He said angrily, his nostrils flaring.

"You're the one not fucking listening." I said, producing the gun from behind my back and aiming it between his eyes. "He's not fucking here."

The man actually smiled at me. And if I wasn't about to piss myself I would've taken more time to admire his very white very straight teeth surrounded by very full lips. But it was the way he smiled with his eyes, an evil glare radiating from his iris's that made even his smile scary.

"Go ahead and shoot," he said, grabbing the barrel of the gun and pressing it to his forehead. "You don't have the balls, girl" he taunted, still smiling.

I mirrored his sarcastic smile and was about to squeeze the trigger when Jake's voice stopped me. "Her balls are bigger than yours, man." Jake side-stepped the stranger and joined me in the entry way.

"I see that now." The man replied, sounding more annoyed than afraid.

"Who the fuck is this guy?" I asked Jake. He took the gun from my hand and placed it back in the drawer. "This is Abby, my wife. Abby, this is..."

The man interrupted.

"They call me, King."

Jake

Brantley King had a dirty cop problem.

Not that the notorious gun runner had anything morally against dirty cops, they just weren't on his side of dirty. A few of the fuckers actually made the mistake of going up against him. They either had balls bigger than grapefruits or were truly the stupidest mother fuckers on the planet.

I didn't care either way.

I had a job to do.

Not that I was going to get back into wet work full time,

but just this little taste should hold me over for a while and keep me home in bed with Bee at night.

And there was no place on earth I'd rather fucking be, then in bed with that girl.

Logan Beach was just a two hour ride north so it didn't take me long before I was burying one of King's problems in the woods.

Well, parts of his problem.

It felt so good to welcome the devil back, even if just for a short time. I felt so fucking good in fact that I found myself humming as I finished covering the last hole, patting down the dirt with the flat side of a shovel before covering it with brush and branches.

I lit a cigarette.

Pure satisfaction coursed through my veins.

My cell rang.

"Yeah."

"Brotha, you still around?" King boomed through the phone. "I got a situation here I could use your help with."

"Yeah man, what you need?"

"Gotta put the fear of God into some piece of shit."

"Done." I said, flipping my phone shut. I took a deep drag and blew the smoke into the night.

I put the last of the brush I'd gathered on top of the freshly packed dirt. When I stood back I couldn't help but smile.

Life is good.

KING

COMING SOON

The day I got out of prison I was tattooing a pussy on a pussy. The animal onto the female part.

A cat on a cunt.

Fucking ridiculous.

The walls of my makeshift tattoo shop pulsed with the heavy beats of the techno music coming from the biker party raging on the floor below, shaking the door as if someone were rhythmically trying to beat it down. Spray paint and posters covered the walls from floor to ceiling, casting a layer of false light over everything within.

If those bikers weren't so vital in my new plan I would have tossed them out hours before. But the truth was that I needed them more than I cared to admit.

The little dark haired bitch I was working on was moaning like she was getting off. I'm sure she was rollin' because there was no way a tattoo directly above her clit could be anything other than fucking painful.

I really needed a different hobby because this one was becoming annoying as fuck. Back in the day I could just zone out for hours while tattooing, finding that little corner of my life that didn't involve all the bullshit I had to deal with on a daily fucking basis. It didn't help that the tattoos people were requesting were becoming fucking dumber and dumber. Football team logos, quotes from books you know they've never read, and wannabe gangsters wanting tear drops on their faces. In prison the tear drop tattoo represented taking a life. Some of these little bitches probably couldn't step on a roach without cowering in the corner and crying for their mamas.

But since my cliental consisted mostly of bikers, strippers, and the occasional spring breaker that found themselves on the wrong side of the causeway, I should've lowered the bar on my expectations.

When I was done with the purple cartoon cat tattoo, I applied vaseline, covered it with wrap, and disposed of my gloves. Did this girl think that guys would be turned on by this thing? It was good work, if I didn't say so myself, especially for being out of commission for three years, but it was covering up my favorite part of a woman. If I undressed her and saw it...I would flip her over.

Which sounded like a good idea.

Instead of giving her instructions for its care and sending her back into the party, I roughly grabbed her hips and pulled her down the table toward me. I stood and flipped her over onto her stomach, with one hand on the back of her neck I pushed her head down onto the table and undid my belt and fly with the other.

She didn't have any money...I didn't do free.

I took her pussy as payment for her new tattoo...of a pussy.

Fuck my life.

She had a great body, but after a few minutes of irritating over-the-top moaning she wasn't doing it for me, not even close, so I grabbed her throat with both hands and squeezed, picking up my pace, taking out my frustrations with each rough thrust in rhythm with the heavy beats from the other room.

Nothing.

I almost didn't notice the door opening.

Almost.

Staring up from my doorway was a large but vacant pair of blue eyes framed by long straight icy-blonde hair, a small dimple in the middle of her chin, a frown on her full pink lips. A girl, no older than seventeen or eighteen, a bit skinny, a bit haunted.

I didn't even realize I was still pumping into the brunette, my orgasm taking me by complete surprise. Closing my eyes, I blew my load into pussy tattoo and collapsed onto her back.

What the fuck?

When I looked back up to the doorway, the doe-eyed girl was gone.

I'm fucking losing my mind.

I rolled out of and off the brunette who was luckily still breathing, although unconscious from either strangulation or the dope that had made her pupils as big as her fucking eye sockets.

I sat back on my rolling stool and put my head in my hands.

I had a massive fucking headache.

It was supposed to be my coming home party, and earlier in the evening I was ready to snort blow of the tits of strippers, but now? Now I just wanted a good nights sleep and these fucking people to get the fuck out of my house.

"You okay, boss-man?" Preppy asked, his head peeking through the opening of the door.

I gestured to the unconscious girl in the chair. "Come get this bitch out of here." I ran my hand through my hair. "And turn this shit down!"

"You got it." Preppy slid past me and didn't question the half naked girl on the table. He hoisted her limp body over his shoulder in one easy movement and made his way back out into the hallway. The unconscious girl's arms flailed around on his back, smacking against random people with each step. Before he could get too far, he turned back to me. "You done with this?" he asked. I could barley hear him over the music, but I could read his lips. He gestured with his chin to the brunette on his shoulder, a child-like grin on his face.

I nodded and Preppy smiled like I'd just told him he could have a puppy, disappearing through the crowd.

Sick fuck.

I loved that kid.

I closed the door, grabbed my gun and knife from the bottom drawer of the tool box I kept my tattoo equipment in, sheathing my knife in my boot and my gun in the waistband of my jeans.

I shook my head from side to side to clear away the haze, prison will do that to you. I hadn't had a good night sleep in three years. Three fucking years sleeping with one eye open in a prison full of people I've made both friends and enemies with over the years.

It was time to keep some of those friends.

Sleep could wait. It was time to party with the bikers. I'd been avoiding doing business with them in any capacity for years. In the past they've been sloppy, slow, and a hindrance. If I didn't need them so fucking badly I wouldn't have even bothered. Money used to be something disposable for me, something I just used to fund my 'I don't give a fuck' lifestyle. But now?

Now I needed it.

A lot of it.

And very fucking soon.

ABOUT THE AUTHOR

T.M. Frazier resides in sunny Southwest Florida with her husband and young daughter. When she's not writing she loves talking to her readers, country music, reading, and traveling. Her debut novel, The Dark Light of Day was published in September of 2013. Dark Needs, a companion novella to The Dark Light of Day was published in February of 2015. She is currently working on her next title, KING. Visit her at www.tmfrazier.com or email her traceymfrazier@gmail.com

CPSIA information can be obtained at www.ICGtesting.com
Printed in the USA
BVOW08s0258050116

431746BV00007B/71/P